Atlanta Smiles

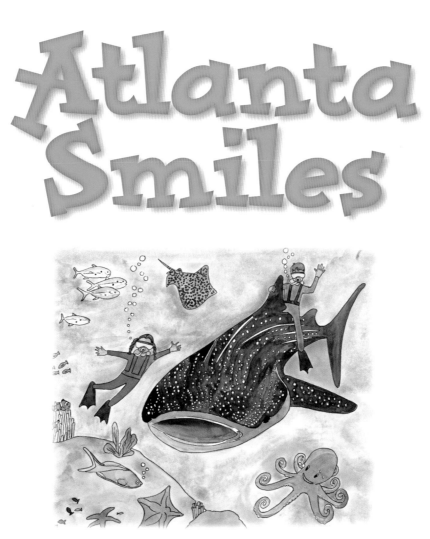

By Angie Smith Patnode & Mary Holcomb McGuire

Illustrated by Kathryn Truluck Krogh

Edited by Caroline Coleman Bennett

Published by:
B.A. Reader Publishing Company, 2 New Grant Court, Columbia, SC 29209   www.bareader.com

First Edition 2011

Printed in the U.S.A. by R. L. Bryan Company.
Cover and Book Layout by Kathryn Truluck Krogh, Krogh Design

Summary: Atlanta native James shows his neighbor's visiting granddaughter, Addie, all the reasons to love Georgia's capital city.
Library of Congress Control Number: 2011903990
ISBN 978-0-9793808-1-5

Illustrations were done in pen and ink and watercolor on illustration board.
This book is set in Improv ICG for headlines and 16pt Comic Sans for body text.

Atlanta Smiles
by Angie Smith Patnode and Mary Holcomb McGuire
Illustrated by Kathryn Truluck Krogh

Dedications

To my mother for passing on her love of children's literature; to my entire family for teaching me to love my home and to always strive to make it a better place; and to Mary - thanks for all the laughs. And especially to my husband, always my biggest cheerleader, and to my two boys for their adventurous spirits. I love you all.

– Angie Smith Patnode

To Mom and Dad for love, encouragement and a happy home; to Angie - nobody could fill your shoes; and to Caleb for making life's everyday adventures the best. I love you.

– Mary Holcomb McGuire

To the Lord for His abundant blessings; to my children, Chandler, Harris and Anna, for bringing me so much joy and love; to my mom, Kay, and dad, Charles, for loving and supporting me in everything I do and for always believing in me; to my sister, Sarah, and brother, Chuck, for always being there for me; to Karen for sharing her love of painting with me.

– Kathryn Truluck Krogh

Acknowledgements

Special thanks go to our late granddad James "J.W." Derrick, who was the perfect model for "James," because he was the perfect model of Southern hospitality; to Addie Johnson, our sister, whose sunny outlook inspired our "Addie"; to Caroline for her kind, patient, generous and endless mentorship; to Kathryn - we couldn't have asked for a better team player; and to Cheryl Sigmon for her reviews and advice. Many thanks also to Steve and Indy Cesari, Julie Ruck, Mark Banta, Dr. Vic Pentz, Dr. Marnie Crumpler and Dr. Brett Jacobson for their vision, guidance and friendship.

In his Atlanta backyard, on a warm day in spring...
while listening to stories the Brown Thrashers sing...
James climbs to the top of his live oak tree.
The school year has ended, and James feels free!

1

Miss Millie walks next door to his green, grassy yard.
She asks for a favor and says, "It won't be hard....
My granddaughter Addie is coming down
to spend the summer. Can you show her around?"

James likes the idea of making a new friend.
He hops from the tree and feels eager to begin.
Being an Atlantan fills James with pride.
"I'll show her the Capital! I'll be her tour guide!"

"**A**tlanta has its share of parks galore
and neighbors to play with right next door.

With so many choices, where should we start?
We could head to the **High Museum**, full of beautiful art.
The splashes of color, carved wood and stone
will inspire us to create a cool piece of our own.

And **Cyclorama** is a place we simply must see....
We will sit in the center of Civil War history!
The world's largest painting fills every wall.
The Battle of Atlanta! We're in the middle of it all!

Another Capital spot that will surely impress:
Center for Puppetry Arts, the largest in the U.S.!
Puppets controlled by shadows, strings or hands
will take us on journeys to faraway lands."

CYCLORAMA

PARKS

ATLANTA
CYCLORAMA
★A CIVIL WAR MUSEUM★

HIGH
HIGH
MUSEUM
OF ART
ATLANTA

CENTER FOR
PUPPETRY
Arts

6

Hartsfield-Jackson **Airport** is her first site,
as Addie meets Atlanta on her jet flight.

She brightly smiles and says, "I'm ready for fun!"
when they step out into the warm Georgia sun.

"Right here," says James, "in the city of my birth,
sits the busiest airport anywhere on Earth."

8

"**H**op in the car, and we're on our way
to another adventurous site for the day."

Cars and semis zoom by like a race;
buses and fire trucks quicken the pace.

Amazed, Addie wonders, "How do they function,
bumper to bumper on **Spaghetti Junction?**"

She points to the **MARTA**®, speeding by on its track.
"It sounds like a roller coaster — Clickety-Clack."

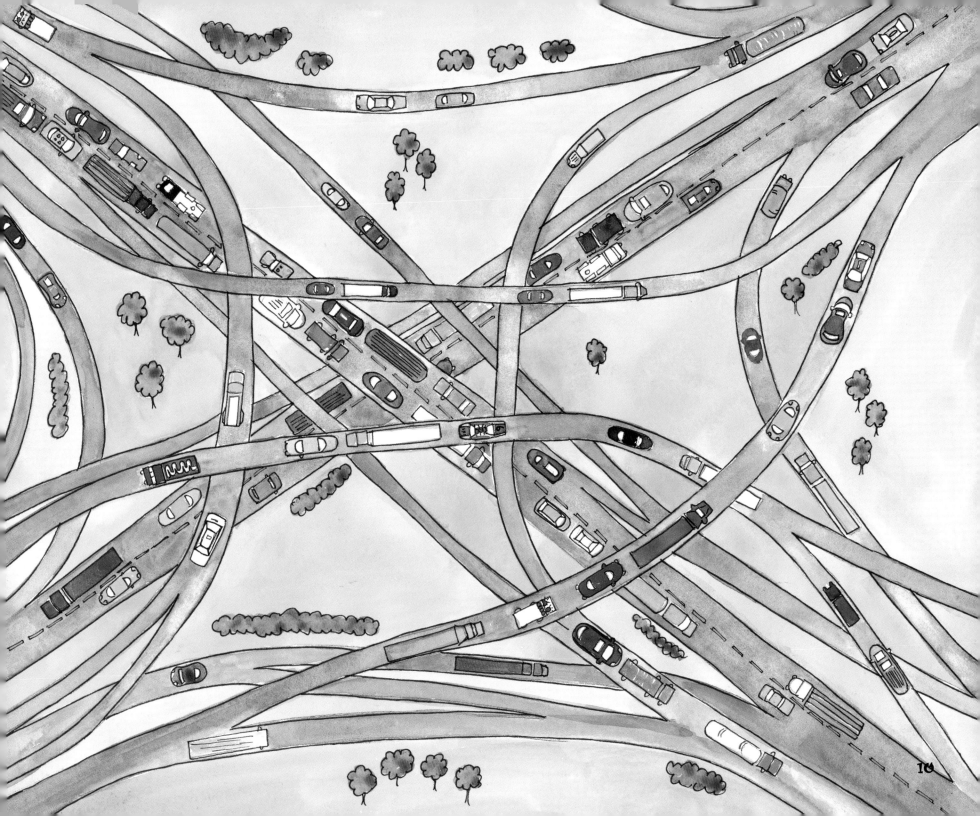

Back at home, James urges, "Addie, come with me!
I have a backyard hideout for you to see."
They stop at a wall of azaleas in bloom,
then dive between buds into his outdoor room.

"To explore my city, we'll have to move fast.
The days will fly, and summer will be in the past.
Grab a paper and pen! We've no time to rest.
You'll soon see that Atlanta is the world's best!
We'll write a checklist of the most fun things to do,
so you can be an Atlanta Adventurer, too."

This city among trees — feel its heartbeat. Adventures are waiting on every street.

The pulse of Atlanta beats in my soul. Let's see my Atlanta! I'm ready to roll!

12

"**N**ow it's time to set sail! Out to blue, rocking seas we go....
Dive through **Georgia Aquarium** to the ocean floor below.

We are sea captains on waters both arctic and warm
to spy dolphins as they dance and watch whale sharks perform.

Feel the belly of this stingray and that shark's pointed fin.
This aquarium has more sea life than any place I've been!"

Glancing at her checklist, Addie asks James,
"Is it true Atlanta once hosted the Olympic Games?

At **Centennial Olympic Park**, it would never get old
to imagine that I've won America a gold!"

James' smile widens and his kind heart sings,
as his friend twirls and whirls in the Fountain of Rings.

This city among trees — feel its heartbeat. Adventures are waiting on every street.

The pulse of Atlanta beats in my soul. Let's see my Atlanta! I'm ready to roll!

16

ZOO ATLANTA

"**G**orillas, rhinos, meerkats and more:
Zoo Atlanta is at our back door!

We'll ride on the carousel, then grab a seat on the train.
Let's roam with zebras and giraffes through the African Plains."

17

18

IMAGINE IT! CHILDREN'S MUSEUM OF ATLANTA

"**A**nother great place to laugh, learn and discover is the **Imagine It! Children's Museum** — the next spot to uncover. I'm an artist, a grocer, a gardener underground... a fireman or crane operator, moving boulders around."

FERNBANK MUSEUM *of* NATURAL HISTORY

"**A**t Fernbank Museum — we'll stand with mouths open wide, as we marvel at the dinosaur bones towering inside.

We'll see a thrilling scene of the giant reptiles clashing: their claws ready to fight and their eight-inch teeth gnashing."

For lunch, James and Addie move toward their mission
to find a delicious Atlanta tradition.

F.O., onion rings, a Naked Dog Walkin'...
Know what you want, and do some fast talkin'.

"What'll ya have? What'll ya have?" a red hat asks Addie.
It's time for a yummy lunch at Atlanta's **Varsity**.

THE VAR

"**L**et's watch hockey with the **Thrashers** or **Hawks** in basketball... homeruns with the **Braves** or **Falcons'** touchdowns in football.

We can eat hot, boiled peanuts 'til we've had our fill, while cheering for the home team — It's all such a thrill!

Hall of Famer Hank Aaron: Do you know this Atlanta Brave? He hit 755 homeruns and made the folks rave.

We can't miss **Atlanta Motor Speedway**: the roar of the crowd, speeding cars, smoking tires, engines so loud!"

"**N**ow let's travel back in time to walk through Georgia history.
We'll learn the settlers' way of life and experience their story."

James knows in the heart of Buckhead stands their passport to the past.
Atlanta History Center makes hands-on learning a blast!

On the battlefield, they pack haversacks and write letters home.
On the farm, they tend gardens and bake biscuits on their own.

FRANKLIN
TREE

From back in the past to up in the sky —
James and Addie twist and turn so high
down Canopy Walk through leafy clouds of green,
40 feet above a magical woodlands scene.

"Have you ever seen snowballs falling in June,
or laughed in a Laugh Garden all afternoon?
Have you tromped under a chrysalis or by a Soggy Bog,
or found yourself to be the target of a poison dart frog?"

In **Atlanta's Botanical Gardens**, Addie remains impressed.
She walks through themed gardens like a princess,
dancing and prancing through a wonderland of blooms.
It's an outdoor castle, full of blossoming rooms!

This city among trees — feel its heartbeat. Adventures are waiting on every street.

The pulse of Atlanta beats in my soul. Let's see my Atlanta! I'm ready to roll!

28

"**W**hat's next on our checklist? We're reaching our goal!
Atlanta Adventurers play a very big role.
We must learn about our city and share it with friends
to lead our Atlanta, where adventures never end.

Our city takes pride in leaders — today's and those from days of old.
So, on to the **King Center**, where a past hero's story unfolds.
Dr. Martin Luther King Jr. led the noble fight
to make sure every American has equal rights.

At the **Presidential Library of Jimmy Carter**, you'll see
what it's like to hold the Number One job in our great country.
Today's leaders buzz around steps of marble and columns of stone
to set Georgia's state laws, beneath the golden **Capitol dome**."

"**N**ext, let's roll out to **Stone Mountain Park**.
We can pack a picnic just before dark,
or hike the trails in the great outdoors,
or watch the laser show. The choice is yours!"

31

This city among trees — feel its heartbeat. Adventures are waiting on every street.

The pulse of Atlanta beats in my soul. Let's see my Atlanta! I'm ready to roll!

The hot Georgia sun starts sinking behind trees
and fireflies ride in on the warm night's breeze.

Addie is drawn to their bright, inner glow
and chases the fireflies who invite her to follow.

Much like an Atlanta Adventurer, they shine
for neighbors and friends to follow behind.

Addie glances at her checklist of all she'd done
since she first met James, and vacation had just begun.

Finding fun in Atlanta, she learns, isn't hard,
whether you tour the sites or play in your backyard.

Atlantans like James strive to make those smile
who visit only a day or stay for a while.

When someone brand new is welcomed like a friend,
she'll only want to come back and visit again.

Georgia State Symbols

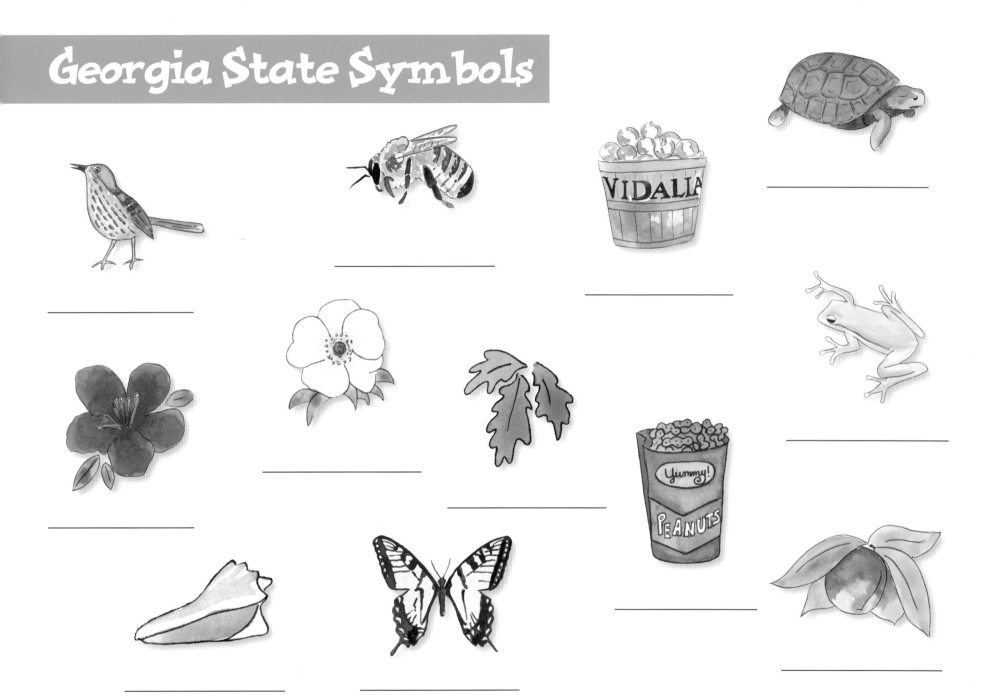

Do you know Georgia's State Symbols?

Glance through Atlanta Smiles, then write the page number(s) on which each is found.

State Amphibian- ______________________

State Bird- ______________________

State Wildflower- ______________________

State Marine Mammal- ______________________

State Butterfly- ______________________

State Fruit- ______________________

State Insect- ______________________

State Flower- ______________________

State Prepared Food- ______________________

State Fish- ______________________

State Crop- ______________________

State Tree- ______________________

State Vegetable- ______________________

State Reptile- ______________________

State Game Bird- ______________________

State Seashell- ______________________

State Gem- ______________________

State Fossil- ______________________

State Mineral- ______________________

State Agriculture- ______________________

State Folk Dance- ______________________

State Song- ______________________

Research all Georgia State Symbols, and look on our web site, www.BAreader.com, for the answers.

Atlanta Adventurer Checklist

Become an Atlanta Adventurer like James and Addie! Just explore our city, and check off each adventure as you complete it. When you've completed at least 15, you can join the Atlanta Adventurers Club. Check our web site, www.BAreader.com, for details.

- [ ] Climb a live oak tree
- [ ] Listen to Brown Thrasher's song
- [ ] Help out a neighbor
- [ ] Have a picnic at Piedmont Park
- [ ] Pick your favorite painting at High Museum
- [ ] See the world's largest painting at Cyclorama
- [ ] Watch Center for Puppetry Arts show
- [ ] Smell an azalea or Cherokee Rose
- [ ] Cruise along Spaghetti Junction
- [ ] Visit Hartsfield-Jackson Airport or ride MARTA®
- [ ] Listen to "Georgia on My Mind"
- [ ] Eat a peach or boiled peanuts
- [ ] Visit the touch tank at Georgia Aquarium
- [ ] Run through fountains at Centennial Olympic Park

- [ ] Control the crane at Imagine It! Children's Museum
- [ ] Cheer on an Atlanta pro team
- [ ] Explore history at Atlanta History Center
- [ ] Discover ancient creatures at Fernbank
- [ ] See the laser show at Stone Mountain
- [ ] Roam with African animals at Zoo Atlanta
- [ ] Eat at The Varsity
- [ ] Enjoy the view from Canopy Walk
- [ ] Listen to the Chattahoochee River
- [ ] Squish your toes in red clay
- [ ] Learn about making peaceful change at King Center
- [ ] Catch fireflies
- [ ] Visit the capitol building
- [ ] Take your picture in the oval office

Other Atlanta Favorites

Studio tour at CNN Center	Dunwoody Nature Center
Philips Arena **PHILIPS** ARENA	Football at Georgia Tech
Margaret Mitchell House	Sweet Auburn Curb Market
The Fox Theatre	Tellus Science Museum
Chattahoochee Nature Center	Marietta Museum of History
Dobbins Air Reserve Base	Six Flags Over Georgia and Six Flags White Water
The Wren's Nest	Kennesaw Mountain National Battlefield Park
Michael C. Carlos Museum, Emory	The Pink Pig at Lenox Square

About the Authors

Angie Smith Patnode

Mary Holcomb McGuire

Angie and Mary are sisters, friends and writing partners. They were inspired to create this book because of their passion for childhood literacy. Angie lives in Atlanta, GA, with Steve, her husband of 11 years. They have two boys, Clayton (9) and Cooper (7), who are always up for more adventures in the Atlanta area! Mary is enjoying newlywed life with her husband, Caleb, in Dallas, TX, where she also teaches first grade.

About the Illustrator

Kathryn Truluck Krogh

About the Publisher

Caroline Coleman Bennett

Kathryn lives in Roswell, a suburb of Atlanta, GA, with her three children, Chandler (15), Harris (13) and Anna (9). Kathryn has loved drawing and painting for as long as she can remember. She graduated from the University of Georgia in Graphic Design and owns her own business, Krogh Design.

Caroline is the owner of B.A. Reader Publishing Company and author of **Charley's Columbia Backyard**, which was named the "Official Children's Book of Columbia" in 2006. Through her company, she strives to help children and families learn about and appreciate their capital cities. A native South Carolinian, she is a graduate of Clemson University, where she met **Atlanta Smiles** partner, Angie Patnode. Caroline is married to Zeke Bennett of Columbia, and together they have three children, Coleman (12), Anna Young (10) and William (8).